W9-AOT-673

Dear Parents:

Congratulations! Your child is taking the first steps on an exciting journey. The destination? Independent reading!

STEP INTO READING® will help your child get there. The program offers five steps to reading success. Each step includes fun stories and colorful art or photographs. In addition to original fiction and books with favorite characters, there are Step into Reading Non-Fiction Readers, Phonics Readers and Boxed Sets, Sticker Readers, and Comic Readers—a complete literacy program with something to interest every child.

Learning to Read, Step by Step!

Ready to Read   Preschool–Kindergarten
• big type and easy words • rhyme and rhythm • picture clues
For children who know the alphabet and are eager to begin reading.

Reading with Help   Preschool–Grade 1
• basic vocabulary • short sentences • simple stories
For children who recognize familiar words and sound out new words with help.

Reading on Your Own   Grades 1–3
• engaging characters • easy-to-follow plots • popular topics
For children who are ready to read on their own.

Reading Paragraphs   Grades 2–3
• challenging vocabulary • short paragraphs • exciting stories
For newly independent readers who read simple sentences with confidence.

Ready for Chapters   Grades 2–4
• chapters • longer paragraphs • full-color art
For children who want to take the plunge into chapter books but still like colorful pictures.

STEP INTO READING® is designed to give every child a successful reading experience. The grade levels are only guides; children will progress through the steps at their own speed, developing confidence in their reading. The F&P Text Level on the back cover serves as another tool to help you choose the right book for your child.

Remember, a lifetime love of reading starts with a single step!

Visit us on the Web!
StepIntoReading.com
randomhouse.com/kids
Educators and librarians, for a variety of teaching tools,
visit us at RHTeachersLibrarians.com

Library of Congress Cataloging-in-Publication Data
Lionni, Leo, 1910–1999, author, illustrator.
Frederick / Leo Lionni.
p. cm. — (Step into reading. Step 3)
"Originally published in hardcover in the United States by Alfred A. Knopf in 1967"—Copyright page.
Caldecott Honor Book, 1968.
Summary: Frederick, the poet mouse, stores up something special for the long cold winter.
ISBN 978-0-385-75549-8 (pbk.) — ISBN 978-0-385-75550-4 (lib. bdg.)
[1. Mice—Fiction.] I. Title.
PZ7.L6634Fo 2014 [E]—dc23 2013038803

This book has been officially leveled by using the F&P Text Level Gradient™ Leveling System.

Printed in the United States of America   10 9 8 7 6 5 4 3 2 1

Frederick

by Leo Lionni

Random House 🏠 New York

All along the meadow

where the cows grazed

and the horses ran,

there was an old stone wall.

5

In that wall, not far
from the barn and the granary,
a chatty family of field mice
had their home.

But the farmers had
moved away,
the barn was abandoned,
and the granary stood empty.
And since winter
was not far off, the little mice
began to gather corn and nuts
and wheat and straw.
They all worked day and night.
All—except Frederick.

"Frederick, why don't you
    work?" they asked.
"I *do* work," said Frederick.
"I gather sun rays
    for the cold dark winter days."

11

And when they saw Frederick
sitting there,
staring at the meadow,
they said, "And now, Frederick?"

"I gather colors,"
  answered Frederick simply.
"For winter is gray."

And once

Frederick seemed half asleep.

"Are you dreaming, Frederick?"

they asked reproachfully.

But Frederick said,

"Oh no, I am gathering words.

"For the winter days
    are long and many,
    and we'll run out
    of things to say."

The winter days came,
and when the first snow fell
the five little field mice
took to their hideout
in the stones.

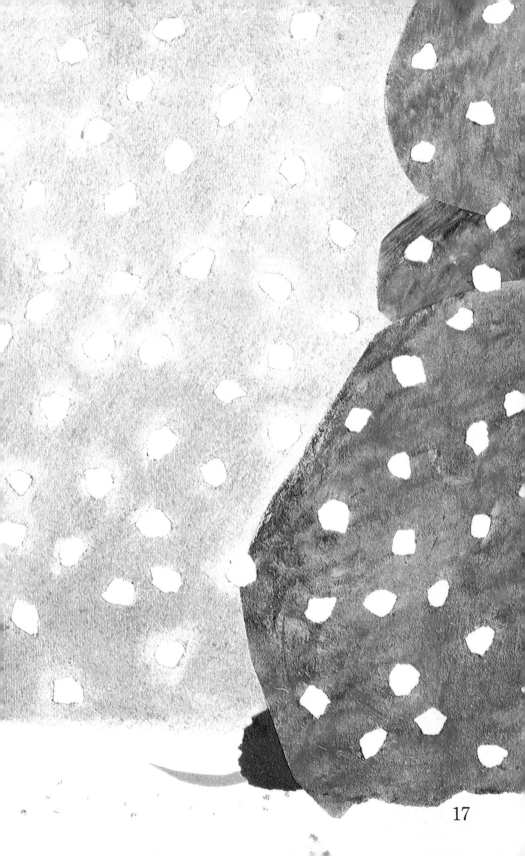

In the beginning
there was lots to eat,
and the mice told stories
of foolish foxes and silly cats.
They were a happy family.

19

But little by little
they had nibbled up
most of the nuts and berries,
the straw was gone,
and the corn was only
a memory.

It was cold in the wall
and no one felt like chatting.

21

Then they remembered
what Frederick had said
about sun rays and
colors and words.

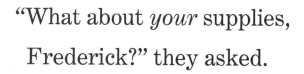

"What about *your* supplies,
Frederick?" they asked.

23

"Close your eyes,"
   said Frederick,
   as he climbed on a big stone.
"Now I send you
   the rays of the sun.
   Do you feel how their
   golden glow . . ."

And as Frederick spoke
of the sun
the four little mice
began to feel warmer.
Was it Frederick's voice?
Was it magic?

"And how about the colors,
　　Frederick?"
　　they asked anxiously.
"Close your eyes again,"
　　Frederick said.
　　And when he told them
　　of the blue periwinkles,
　　the red poppies
　　in the yellow wheat,

and the green leaves of the
berry bush, they saw the colors
as clearly as if they had been
painted in their minds.

"And the words, Frederick?"
Frederick cleared his throat,
waited a moment, and then,
as if from a stage, he said:

"Who scatters snowflakes?
Who melts the ice?
Who spoils the weather?
Who makes it nice?
Who grows the
four-leaf clovers in June?
Who dims the daylight?
Who lights the moon?
Four little field mice who live
in the sky. Four little
field mice . . . like you and I.

'One is the Springmouse
who turns on the showers.
Then comes the Summer
who paints in the flowers.
The Fallmouse is next
with walnuts and wheat.
And Winter is last . . .
with little cold feet. Aren't we
lucky the seasons are four?
Think of a year with one less . . .
or one more!"

When Frederick had finished,
they all applauded.
"But Frederick," they said,
"you are a poet!"
Frederick blushed, took a bow,
and said shyly, "I know it."

LEO LIONNI wrote and illustrated
more than forty picture books in his
lifetime, including four Caldecott Honor
Books—*Inch by Inch, Swimmy, Frederick,*
and *Alexander and the Wind-Up Mouse.*
He died in 1999 at the age of 89.

Praise for Leo Lionni

"If the picture book is a new visual art form in our time, Leo Lionni is certain to be judged a master of the genre."

—Selma Lanes, *The New York Times*

Guess the Word

How well do you know *Frederick*?
Can you remember the story
by reading the sentences below?

This story is about a named
Frederick.

Frederick and the other mice are getting
ready for

.

The mice gather  so they
will be prepared.

But Frederick gathers words.
When it snows, the mice hide in a

 .

In the winter, Frederick helps the mice feel
warm and see .

The poem in this story is about the
four seasons.

Seasons

In this story, the mice get ready
for winter. Do you know
all four seasons? Which season
matches each picture?

spring   summer
fall   winter

What doesn't belong?

Do you remember the pictures from
the story? Which one is different
from the rest?

Alexander is a real mouse, but everyone loves Willy, the wind-up mouse. Can Alexander become a wind-up mouse, too?